Fergus and Bridey

Olivier Dunrea

BRUN

A Dell Picture Yearling Book

Published by
Dell Publishing
a division of
Bantam Doubleday Dell Publishing Group, Inc.
666 Fifth Avenue
New York, New York 10103

ISBN: 0-440-40691-9

Reprinted by arrrangement with the author

Printed in the United States of America
September 1992
10 9 8 7 6 5 4 3 2 1

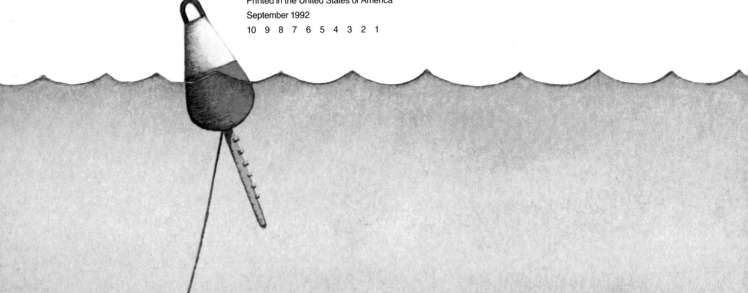

For KRISTIN, *who swims in the birdbath*

This is Fergussen og Snorren. Fergus for short.

This is Bridey Mor McPherson. Bridey for short.

They live by the edge of the sea.

One day, Fergus and Bridey find an old treasure map
in a bottle.

"Well, Bridey," says Fergus, "it's off to find treasure!"

"Rowf," replies Bridey.

Dead man's island
Dragon spine skerries
Here the treasure is hid
carved stone
walk 10 paces
stone Circle
Shark waters
Dismal Swamp
North

They put everything they need for the voyage in their
boat. They pack a big black umbrella, two oars, nine
tins of sea biscuits, a red ball, a telescope, a shovel,
four wax candles, a box of matches, a flask of water,
and, of course, *the* map.

And off they go.

Fergus rows the boat while Bridey eats sea biscuits.
It's such a fine day, Fergus goes for a swim. Bridey
watches for pirates and sharks. Suddenly, a huge fin
comes toward them.

Bridey barks loudly, and Fergus scrambles into the boat.
"Phew," he says, "that was close."

He rows the boat furiously.

That night, they sleep peacefully as the boat rocks
gently on the calm sea.

The next morning is bright and sunny. Fergus fishes
while Bridey sits under the umbrella.

Fergus doesn't catch anything, but Bridey snatches a fish with her mouth. She loses her balance and falls overboard with a loud splash!

"Watch out for sharks!" warns Fergus.

Bridey bolts out of the water, back into the boat.

The sea becomes choppy, and Bridey becomes seasick.
The sky grows gray. The wind whistles loudly.
"Looks like a bad storm's brewing," says Fergus. "Better
hang on tight." Bridey shivers in the bottom of the boat.

The waves toss the boat back and forth. Lightning
flashes and rain pours down on the two friends.

The storm ends quickly. Just as they think they're safe,
a gigantic wave flings the boat out of the water.

Bridey is lost overboard!

"Bridey!" shouts Fergus. "Bridey, where are you?"
Bridey doesn't answer.

Fergus leans over the side. He sees a little black nose.

He reaches out and pulls Bridey into the boat.
He holds her tight, and Bridey licks his face.

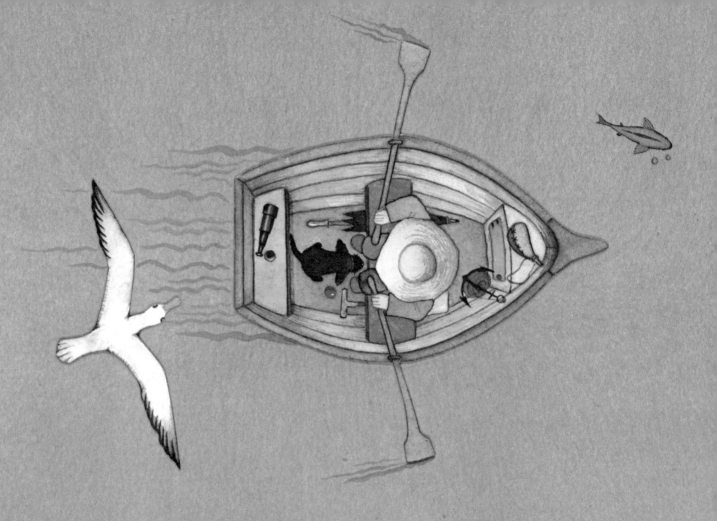

"Well, Bridey, do you still want to find that treasure?"
asks Fergus.

Bridey smiles and wags her tail.

Fergus takes out the map and studies it. "We're almost there," he says.

Bridey stretches and yawns.

"Look!" shouts Fergus. "There's the island."
Fergus rows the boat toward the island and throws
the anchor overboard.

The two friends wade ashore.

"There's the carved stone that's on the map," says
Fergus excitedly. "Now we walk ten paces and start
digging!"

"1-2-3-4-5-6-7-8-9-10!" he counts as they reach the spot where the treasure is hidden. They dig and dig. Finally they hit something hard in the sand. "This must be it!" yells Fergus.

They uncover a small wooden chest.

Fergus holds his breath and carefully opens the lid.
Inside the chest is a small gold ring.
"It's beautiful," whispers Fergus. Bridey sniffs
the treasure. Fergus puts the ring on Bridey's tail.

"Now we can go home," he says.

And they do.